FISHY BUSINESS FOR
FRANCIS FRY

Sam McBratney
& Kim Blundell

COLOUR JETS

Colour Me Crazy; The Footprints Mystery
Cosmic Kev   Andrew Donkin
Captain Skywriter and Kid Wonder   Stephen Elboz
Dad on the Run   Sarah Garland
Gertie and the Bloop   Julia Jarman
Stinker Muggles and the Dazzle Bug   Elizabeth Laird
Under the Red Elephant   Jan Mark
Francis Fry, Private Eye; Francis Fry and the O.T.G.
Fishy Business for Francis Fry   Sam McBratney
Sick As a Parrot   Michaela Morgan
Harry Fly   Tasha Pym
Aunt Jinksie's Miracle Seeds; Boys Are Us   Shoo Rayner
Even Stevens F.C.   Michael Rosen
Dear Alien   Angie Sage
Reggie the Stuntman   Kate Shannon

First published in paperback in Grea
by HarperCollins Publishers Ltd 199?

The HarperCollins website address is
www.fireandwater.com

10 9 8 7 6 5 4 3

Text © Sam McBratney 1999
Illustrations © Kim Blundell 1999

The author and illustrator assert the moral right to be
identified as the author and illustrator of the work.

A CIP record for this title is available from the British Library.

ISBN 0 00 675382 5

Printed and Bound by Printing Express Ltd., Hong Kong.

Chapter 1

Hi. Welcome to my new office. It's a conservatory - very warm and bright.

This afternoon, I had my first customer. I was reading my E-mail when he came in.

Posh accent. In my job it pays to be a good listener. I wondered what the J stood for. John? No, too ordinary, this gent looked more like a Jasper. Or a Jeremiah.

Need your help, Fry. Something urgent has come up. If you're busy, I'll double your normal fee.

Now I wouldn't say I'm greedy, but that kind of talk gets my attention. A new conservatory is not cheap.

Sir Harley handed me a card.

I'll talk to you at
the scene of the crime
tomorrow morning at ten.
Good day to you, Fry.

Sir Harley J. Spendlove
Grand Cedar Lodge

Away he went.
I spun round
twice in my swivel
chair. Double fee,
I thought.
Must be serious.
Maybe even
murder most foul.

6

Then, mouse in hand, I read my E-mail.

Dear Francis Fry Private Eye,

My friend Elizabeth Winterspout
told me that you found her teddy
when a baddie stole it. Somebody
stole both of my fish. Could you
find them for me, please? They
are quite old and they need me
to look after them and I will
always be your friend if you do.

Jamie Bowen, aged 9

My heart sank. Let's face it, goldfish are
small fry. I find missing diamonds,
solve murders, catch spies
– I can't go chasing
after two fish at
the drop of a hat!

On the other hand I'm not good at
saying no to nine-year-old children, so I
took the easy way out. I did nothing.

Chapter 2

Next morning I set off early for Grand Cedar Lodge, but first I had some business to attend to. I had to pay the bill for my new conservatory.

Stanley Beakwell

Garden Centre

Homes and Gardens
Landscaping
Tree Surgery
Conservatories

An old friend of mine called Stanley Beakwell had sold it to me. We'd both gone to the same school, Beaky and me. We wanted to be tree surgeons when we grew up. Happy days!

Beaky owns a garden centre at the edge of town. He's done quite well for himself with his big house and its indoor swimming pool.

We talked about old times and I gave Beaky a cheque. Parting with money is always painful, but let me tell you – writing all those noughts was agony.

Then I drove to the scene of the crime.

As yet I knew
nothing about the
crime, of course, but the
scene was quite something!
Sir Harley J Spendlove lived in a
mansion. Mighty cedars of Lebanon
lined the long drive to the front door.
Very pretty.

A blue van at the front of the house belonged to Winston Bright, Window Cleaner. I notice these things; it's my job.

A butler met me at the bottom of the steps.

Smooth sort, that butler. Even his hair was smoothed flat to the skull. I've been to many places and seen many things, but this was my first actual butler. That moustache looked fake to me.

There is no need to come into the house, Sir. The Master will join you presently at the fountain.

When Sir Harley arrived, I admired his trees.

"Yes," he boomed. "They're nearly two hundred years old. Planted on the day of Lord Nelson's Funeral. Unfortunately we had a little storm damage recently, but nothing too serious."

We walked around the fountain.
The water fell like gentle rain on two
smiling plastic gnomes.

"Should have brought my umbrella,"
I joked, but Sir Harley
did not smile.

Someone is stealing fish from this pool, Fry.

Jumping jackdaws! Fish again.

Sir Harley J Spendlove smiled ever so slightly as he tickled the water with his fingers.

Up from the depths of the pond cruised a mighty speckled creature at least as long as your arm and probably as long as your leg.

A brute like that could eat the heron!

16

"Meet Bentley," Sir Harley said sadly. "He is an ornamental carp, Fry. A koi. They are the kings of the fishy realm. My late father had four of them flown over from Japan years ago."

Then came a thief in the night and now I only have two left. Two! This sort of thing is very distressing. My butler is heartbroken. He feeds them each morning, you see. They were like family to him.

"I see," I said.

17

Just then, the window cleaner arrived for his money. I watched Spendlove write him a cheque for £100. That's a lot of window!

When I pay my window cleaner I expect change from a fiver.

What could I say? Beaky's conservatory had left a crater in my pockets.

"Well, it's not exactly my field, Sir," I replied carefully, "but I shall be glad to make some enquiries."

Chapter 3

I chewed some
liquorice as I drove
home. It helps me
think. Then I walked
to the nearest pet
shop. First things first –
let's find out about fish.

In the pet shop I saw
some live maggots
wriggling in a bowl of
sawdust. I saw a locust being crunched
by a small green dinosaur.

On the top shelf a snake polished off a
mouse. A man on a stool was feeding red
meat to a tank of ravenous piranha fish.
You talk about violence on TV? Somebody
should do something about pet shops.

21

The man on the stool was the owner –
Mr Peacock. I wished him good morning.

So. Bentley's friends didn't die of natural
causes. That's how I work, eliminate the
obvious.

23

Mr Peacock grinned. He had pointy teeth
- a bit like the piranha fish, actually.

Jumping jackdaws!
Nearly one thousand pounds for an
overgrown goldfish! Are people crazy?
For that sort of money I'd expect a whale.

A thief who stole ten big fish could net nearly ten thousand pounds! Think about it.

We were talking serious money here! It was time I paid a visit to a young friend, aged nine years old.

Chapter 4

Jamie Bowen showed me his empty
goldfish pond and it was a sad sight.

"I see," I said,
although this was an exaggeration.

Mother came to the rescue. "With and Without were the names of the fish, Mr Fry," she told me. "Would you like to see a photograph?"

I only have a photo of With, I haven't got one of Without.

With will do.

There he was, orange dot and all. Although no match for Bentley, With was quite a fish.

I asked Mrs Bowen if there had been any visitors to the house on the day of the crime.

It was the day after that big storm, wasn't it, Jamie?

Our tree blew down. My tree house was in it.

I remember the window cleaner came...

A plastic gnome on the pond seemed
to wink at me.

Another blue van. Fish missing from
two ponds. Could this be the same
window cleaner?

On the way out, Jamie Bowen thrust a book and a pencil at me.

Can I have your autograph please, Mr Fry?

I'll do what I can to find your fish, young fellow, but I can't make any promises.

I had a feeling this was going to be tricky.

Chapter 5

It's not hard to find a window cleaner named Bright in the Yellow Pages.

I parked outside his house until the blue van came home.

WINSTON
BRIGHT
WINDOW
CLEANER

Winston Bright himself answered my knock on the door. Hanging round his knees were three happy children and a dog, their mouths smeared with chocolate.

I explained about the missing fish, and the fact that his van had been seen at the scene of two crimes.

Sometimes they get angry when you talk like that, but Winston Bright just sighed.

I saw no sign of water in the van. There was a bucket, true enough, but a monster like Bentley could have worn it for a hat.

While I checked for evidence, Winston Bright watched me with sad eyes.

When I find an open window, Mr Fry, do you know what I do? I close it.

I have an instinct for these things; it comes with the job. Here was no thief. Winston Bright was a closer of open windows and I felt like a heel. Accusing a decent man of being a low criminal is the worst thing you can do.

It was time for me to go and see Charlie, the Chief Inspector down at the police station. I chewed some liquorice on the way, but it tasted like humble pie.

I found Charlie
poised to attack a
double cheeseburger.

Oh dear.
Charlie took a lump out of his
cheeseburger like a lion eating a hyena.

A glance at the computer screen
showed me the size of the problem.
Fish were disappearing everywhere,
even from the town parks. No garden
pond in the city was safe.

37

"I mean, you can't lock up your goldfish pond, can you?" cried Charlie. "The thing won't go in the garage at night!"

I couldn't argue with that.

While I was thinking, a policeman walked by, escorting a man who swayed on his feet. This wild character looked at me and said, "They don't believe me. They think I'm mad."

Why is that, Sir?

"Get that drunken fool outta here!"
yelled Charlie.

I made a print-out of the names on the computer screen, thinking they might be useful. As I left, Charlie finished off his poor cheeseburger.

Chapter 6

It was time to think.

Motive.

Opportunity.

Method.

All the great detectives will tell you that this is the hardest work there is. You have to focus your brain.

The motive I knew. Money.  Second-hand carp were a nice little earner.

Method? There had
to be transport of
some kind,
probably a
specially equipped van.

Opportunity. This
was the problem –
the thief had to know
that someone had a
pond in the garden
with fish in it.
Who might have
that knowledge?

I thought of postmen,
dustmen, milkmen, even
the pilots of light aircraft.

And of course, fish have
to be fed. The owner of
a pet shop would know
who had fish in their
back garden...

I drove to Peacock's Pet Shop, just in case. Sometimes a hunch is all you've got.

Down the street came a figure in a bowler hat. I recognised that moustache. Where was Harley J Spendlove's butler going with that big plastic barrel?

I held my breath and sure enough, he went through the pet shop door. Could Peacock and the butler be in it together?

Sneaking up to the window, I peeped through a cage of canaries and saw them having a natter.

Time to act! I opened the door and quickly went in. Peacock looked surprised to see me, but that butler was a cool customer.

Ah, Mr Fry. Any trace of Phoebe and Galileo?

Phoebe and Galileo, With and Without. What gets into people who keep fish? I mean, what's wrong with Jack and Jill?

"Not yet," I said, looking into the barrel. It was half full of pellets. Nothing sinister there. The butler was simply buying Bentley's breakfast.

I nodded to them both and left the shop with another little thought in my head. Sir Harley J Spendlove had a big house with big bills.

Think about it.

Was he stealing his own fish – for the insurance money?

Stranger things have happened.

46

Chapter 7

The next day I talked to a lot of
sad people about their missing
fish. My feet were sore by the time
I got to the last name on the list: the
Reverend Harold Wise of St Jude's.

> I wish they'd taken my
> TV or my car, and left Adam and
> Eve alone. The children loved to feed
> them. And those fish knew my voice,
> Mr Fry.

I nodded,
but the fact
is, I didn't
know fish
had ears.

I couldn't disagree with that.

I reported back to Charlie that nobody had seen anything strange.

Nobody ever sees nothing! Who's nicking them, then — the invisible man? UFOs?

Things are bad when you start blaming aliens.

"Charlie," I said, "if we can't find the criminal, let's try to keep an eye on the fish. Where are the next likely targets?"

Charlie punched his computer keys.

Thirty-five addresses with ponds. You want to watch them all? You want the whole police force out guarding goldfish?

There wasn't much point in talking to Charlie in this mood so I went back to my office. It was time to chew some liquorice.

Phoebe and Galileo. Adam and Eve. How can fish vanish into thin air?

The more I thought, the worse I felt. Jamie Bowen had my autograph, but he had no Without and he was without With. He was relying on me and I hadn't a clue. The poor little fellow didn't even have his tree house any more.

How long did I sit there before it hit me? I don't know, but all of a sudden I saw it all. Everything! Even Noddy and Big-Ears fell into place.

I made thirty-five phone calls.

After one hour and eleven minutes I had what I wanted to know.

Then I made one more call.

Shake a leg, Charlie. It's Blackstaff Manor. Let's go fishing!

Chapter 8

It was close to sunset when we reached Blackstaff Manor. The pond was the size of a small lake.

And they were there!

Two hunched figures sat in the shallow
water. For all the world they looked like
two garden gnomes, fishing.

"*Somebody* round here is crazy," moaned Charlie. "Plastic gnomes!"

But the gnomes were not plastic, oh no. The fishing rods were real, too. Suddenly a huge fish rose out of the lake, fighting like fury. Gnome 1 had it on the end of his line. Gnome 2 swished it up in a net.

Before you could cry "Enid Blyton" the gnomes raced for the woods, where they'd hidden their van.

There was also the back-up team Charlie and I had called in…

Gnome 1 panicked and tried to run for it, but he didn't get far.

That left Gnome 2.
Close up, he didn't look like a gnome at all. He was wearing rubber boots that came right up to his waist. And a little woolly hat.

I want my lawyer.

Who is this joker, anyway? Do we know him?

"Once I realised the storm damage linked all these crimes, I simply had to find out who was called in to work on the trees," I explained.

Beaky wouldn't tell us where the stolen fish were hidden. Next day Charlie organised a search of the garden centre, but the fish weren't there.
SALE
Maybe he's already sold them! Or perhaps they're dead!
No. I think we'll find them alive and well – in the only other place they can be...

Chapter 9

Back home there was an E-mail message for me.

To Francis Fry, Private Eye.

This is your friend Jamie Bowen. With and Without are swimming about in my pool again. I have fed them food and they are eating it. Thank you very much. I'm glad I got your autograph, Francis Fry.

There was also a present for my new conservatory.

I call them Jack and Jill.

Well done, Fry.
From
Harley Jonah Spendlove